D0403208

THE
SECRET
GARDEN

THE SECRET GARDEN

by
Frances Hodgson Burnett

Abridged, adapted,
and illustrated
by
quadrum■
Quadrum Solutions, Mumbai, India

Modern Publishing
A Division of Kappa Books Publishers, LLC.

Cover art by Quadrum

Contents

CHAPTER 1

There's No One Left

When Mary Lennox arrived at Misselthwaite Manor, everyone thought she was very unpleasant looking. She was quite thin and had a sour expression on her face. She had blond, thin hair and yellowish skin. This was because she was born in India and she was almost always sick.

Her father worked for the English government and was always busy and ill himself. Her mother, a beauty, loved to go to parties. She never wanted a baby girl

and so she handed Mary over to the care of an ayah. The ayah was told to always keep the child out of sight.

The other servants did whatever Mary wanted, for they were sure their memsahib would be angry if she heard Mary crying. By the time Mary was six, she became a spoiled and angry child. The governess, who came to teach her to read and write, disliked her very much; she left after three months. The only reason Mary learned her letters and numbers was because she truly wanted to.

One morning she saw that the woman by her bedside was not her ayah.

"Why have you come?" she asked the strange woman. "Where is my ayah? Send

her to me."

The woman just looked at her, nervously wringing her hands together. She stammered that the ayah would not be able to come. Mary got angry and went out into the garden to play by herself.

She was still there when her mother came out into the veranda with a fair

The Secret Garden

gentleman; he was an officer from England. She stared at her mother, like she always did whenever she had the chance to, for she was indeed beautiful. She was well dressed, tall, and slim, with silky curls and laughing eyes. Mary looked at her eyes and saw, for the first time, fear instead of laughter.

"Is it bad then?" asked Mrs. Lennox.

"Quite awful!" said the officer. "You should have left for the hills weeks ago."

"I only stayed to go to that silly party! What a fool I am!" she lamented.

Suddenly, a loud wail came from the servants' quarters, followed by a few other heartbroken cries. Mrs. Lennox grabbed the officer's arm.

"Someone has just died," she said.

"You did not tell me it broke out amongst your servants, too," said the officer. They rushed inside.

Now Mary understood why her ayah

didn't show up. The cholera had spread across the city like wildfire. The ayah had caught the disease the night before and died that morning.

In all the confusion, Mary was forgotten. No one came to check on her. She crept into the empty dining room and ate all the leftovers. Being thirsty, she finished off a glass of wine not knowing

how strong it was. She soon felt light- headed and went off to sleep for several hours, during which time much happened.

When she woke up, the house was quiet and still. She had never heard absolute silence in this house before. She grew upset, for no one came to see if the cholera had taken her.

Just then, two men entered the house.

"What a tragedy! That pretty woman, and the child, I suppose. I heard there was a child, though I never saw her," exclaimed one of the men.

The other, who Mary recognized as someone she had seen talking to her father once, look tired and worn out. When he saw Mary, he was startled.

"Barney!" he cried. "A child! Alone, in this place! Who is she?"

The girl stood up slowly. "I am Mary Lennox. I fell asleep when everyone had

the cholera, and I just woke up. Why did nobody come for me?"

"It's the child no one saw! She has actually been forgotten!" exclaimed the man.

"Why have I been forgotten?" Mary

stamped her foot on the ground. "Why has no one come for me?"

Barney looked at her sadly as tears fell from his eyes.

"Poor child, there is no one left to come," he said.

In this way, Mary found out that she had lost both her parents to the cholera. The few servants who had not died had left the house in the night. None of them had remembered her. That is why the place was so quiet.

CHAPTER 2

"Mistress Mary Quite Contrary" Arrives at the Manor

Mary was sent to an English clergyman's house. He was poor and had five children who wore dirty clothes and always fought. Mary was rude to them, and they gave her a nickname, which made her furious!

Basil was a little boy with blue eyes and an upturned nose, and Mary hated him. One day, she was playing by herself in the garden when Basil came near her

and watched. She looked at him and cried out, "Go away! I don't like boys, go away!"

For a moment Basil looked angry, but then he just started laughing. He danced around her, singing and making funny faces!

The Secret Garden

"Mistress Mary, quite contrary,
How does your garden grow?
With silver bells, and cockleshells,
And marigolds all in a row."

All the other children laughed. They began calling her Mistress Mary Quite Contrary. Basil told her she was leaving by the end of the week.

"You are going to your uncle. His name is Mr. Archibald Craven," he told her.

"I don't know anything about him," snapped Mary.

"I know you don't," Basil answered. "You don't know anything. I heard Father and Mother talking about him. He lives in a great big old house in the country. He's always cross, and he is a horrid hunchback."

"I don't believe you," said Mary, and she turned her back and stuck her fingers in her ears because she would not listen anymore. But she thought about it a lot.

A woman, Mrs. Medlock, was sent to pick Mary up. She was Mr. Craven's housekeeper at Misselthwaite Manor. She was a stout woman with rosy cheeks and sharp eyes. Mary didn't like her at all!

Mary was very curious about her uncle and the place he lived in. What sort of a place was it, and what would he be like? Mary began wondering why she was so alone, even when her parents had been alive and well. She didn't belong

to anyone. She didn't know that it was because she was mean and rude; she didn't even know she *was* mean and rude. It was something she thought of others.

Mary thought Mrs. Medlock was a very disagreeable-looking woman, with her colored face and her bright bonnet.

Mary sat in a corner of the railway carriage and looked plain and fretful. Her light-colored dress made her look yellower than ever, and her limp, light hair straggled from under her hat. Mrs. Medlock briskly began talking to her.

"I might as well tell you about the manor," she began. "Do you know anything about your uncle?"

"No," Mary replied.

"Didn't your parents talk of him?"

"No."

After a few moments of silence, Mrs. Medlock began again. "The manor is huge and gloomy. Mr. Craven is quite proud of it, though. The house is six hundred years old, on the edge of a moor. About a hundred rooms, though most of them are locked up. There's old furniture that's been there for ages, a big park around the house with trees in it. But there's nothing else!" She ended suddenly.

In spite of herself, Mary listened to her. It didn't sound like India, and anything new attracted her.

"Well, what do you think?" asked Mrs. Medlock.

"Nothing. I know nothing of such places."

"Don't you care?"

"No," replied Mary.

Mrs. Medlock said, "I don't know why

you are even being called there. He won't
have anything to do with you. He's got a
crooked back, Mr. Craven. Only time the
place saw life was when he got married."

Mary was surprised, as she didn't
think hunchbacks got married. Seeing her
reaction, Mrs. Medlock went on. "She was
such a pretty, sweet thing. People thought
she married for money. But she didn't! When

she died . . ."

Mary gave an involuntary jump. "Oh! Did she?" She suddenly felt sorry for Mr. Craven.

"She did. And Mr. Craven became even stranger after that. He won't see people. He doesn't see anyone except old Pitcher. Pitcher has taken care of him since he was a boy, you see."

The whole scenario sounded like a gloomy book, which didn't cheer Mary up one bit.

"Don't expect to see him," said Mrs. Medlock, "and don't expect anyone to talk to you. You'll be told in which rooms you can go and in which you can't. Mr. Craven won't have you poking around his house."

"I will not go poking about," said Mary, immediately regretting feeling sorry for Mr. Craven.

She turned and looked out of the

window at the gray rain clouds and at the drops falling on the window. Her eyes fell slowly, and soon she was fast asleep.

CHAPTER 3

Across the Moor

She woke up to Mrs. Medlock shaking her after the train had stopped at the station.

"Time to wake up," she said. "We've got a long drive ahead of us."

They were the only ones getting off at the small station. The stationmaster spoke to Mrs. Medlock for a few minutes, then informed her that the carriage was just outside.

A brougham stood on the road before the little outside platform. Mary saw that it was a smart carriage and that it was a

smart footman who helped her in. His long waterproof coat and the waterproof covering of his hat were shining and dripping with rain. Mary found herself seated comfortably inside a cushioned corner.

"What is a moor?" she asked Mrs. Medlock suddenly.

"You'll see in ten minutes."

The Secret Garden

Mary quietly looked outside the window. They drove through a tiny village with whitewashed houses. They passed a church, a vicarage, and a tiny toy shop. Finally, the carriage moved slowly, as if moving upward. There were no more hedges or trees. Mary saw nothing but dense darkness on both sides.

"We're surely on the moor now," remarked Mrs. Medlock.

The wind was rising, and it made a whistling sound. "It's . . . it's not the sea, is it?" Mary asked Mrs. Medlock.

"No. Nor is it fields or mountains. Just miles and miles of wild lands that grow nothing but heather and have only wild ponies and sheep living on it."

On and on they drove through the darkness, and though the rain stopped, the wind rushed by and whistled and made strange sounds. Several times the carriage passed over a little bridge, beneath which water rushed very fast with a great deal of noise. Mary felt as if the wide, bleak moor were a wide expanse of black ocean through which she was passing on a strip of dry land.

"I don't like it," she said to herself, and pinched her thin lips more tightly together. The horses were climbing up a hilly piece of road when she first caught sight of a light. Mrs. Medlock saw it as soon as Mary did and drew a long sigh of relief.

"Finally, a little light!" said Mrs. Medlock. "It's the light at the lodge window. In a bit we'll get ourselves a cup of tea."

After a short while they drove through

the park gates, with two more miles to cover before arriving at the house. The avenue of trees made it seem like they were going through a dark tunnel. They came out of the tunnel and stopped outside a very long but low-built house.

The entrance door was huge, made of massive panels of wood studded with nails and bound with iron bars. It opened into an enormous hall that was dimly lit. A neat, thin old man stood near the manservant who opened the door for them.

"You are to take her to her room," he said. "He doesn't want to see her. He's going to London tomorrow."

"Very well, Mr. Pitcher," she said. "I'll see to that."

"See that he isn't disturbed."

Mary Lennox was led up a broad staircase, down a long corridor, up a short flight of steps, and through another corridor and another, until a door opened

The Secret Garden

in a wall and she found herself in a room with a fire in it and supper on a table.

Mrs. Medlock said unceremoniously: "Well, here you are! This room and the next is where you'll live, and you must stay in them. Don't you forget that!"

CHAPTER 4

Martha and the Gardens

When Mary woke up the next morning, she saw a young woman lighting a fire and raking the cinders noisily. She had never seen a gloomy room like this. There was a brilliantly done tapestry that hung on the wall. Mary felt like she was part of the forest scene.

"What is that?" she asked, pointing out of the window.

The young housemaid, Martha, rose to her feet and looked out of the window. "That's the moor. Do you like it?"

"No, I hate it," Mary replied.

Martha continued scrubbing the fireplace. "I love it. There are sweet-smelling things growing around. There's so much fresh air! The sky is clear, and in the summer you see everything in bloom. I wouldn't live away from the moor for

anything."

Mary listened with a puzzled expression. Her servants in India weren't like this. They never spoke to their masters as if they were talking to their own. "You're a strange servant. Are you going to be my servant?" asked Mary as if she were royalty.

"I'm Mrs. Medlock's servant, and she's Mr. Craven's. But I'm here to do some housework and to wait on you a bit. But don't expect much waiting on!"

"Who's going to dress me?"

Martha put her hands on her hips and spoke in a thick Yorkshire accent. "Can't you dress yourself? I mean, can't you put your own clothes on?" she repeated when she realized the child didn't understand her accent.

"No, I never did. My ayah always dressed me," said Mary.

"Well," said Martha, "now's a good

time to learn."

"It was different in India," said Mary, fuming now.

Martha said softly, "When I heard you were coming from India, I thought you would be black."

Mary jumped and stood on her bed and fisted her hands. "How dare you! You thought I was a native? You daughter of a pig!"

Martha looked squarely at her, quite angry herself. "Don't call me names! Why are you so angry? I have nothing against the blacks; in fact, I was quite pleased to think I'd see one up close for the very first time! But when I drew back the sheets this morning to look at you I was quite disappointed. You're more yellow than black."

Mary couldn't stand the humiliation. At that moment she felt so lonely, she threw herself on her pillows facedown and

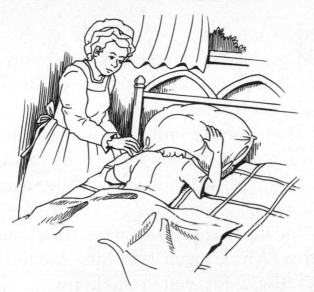

began sobbing passionately. Martha went over to her. "There now, you mustn't cry like that! I didn't know you'd be so angry. I beg your pardon, miss. Please stop crying."

There was something pleasing about the Yorkshire accent. Slowly, Mary stopped crying and Martha looked relieved.

"Time for you to get up now. The room next door has been made into a nursery for you. You're to have your meals there. I'll help you with your clothes if you get out of bed."

Mary got out of bed and saw that the clothes Martha took out from the wardrobe did not belong to her.

"These aren't mine," she told her, looking at the dress with a thick white wool coat. "Mine are black, and these are much nicer."

"You've been told to wear this," said Martha. "Mr. Craven told Mrs. Medlock to get these for you from London. He didn't want a child wandering about in black clothes looking like a lost soul."

She dressed Mary silently. She asked why she didn't put on her own shoes when Mary quietly lifted a foot. "My ayah did it for me—it was the custom."

Martha continued to talk to her as she did her chores. Gradually, Mary relaxed.

She went to the nursery and found it as gloomy as her room. She looked at the heavy breakfast tray and, as she had a small appetite, she looked away.

"I don't want it," she said, frowning.

"You don't want your porridge?" asked Martha, shocked.

Mary shook her head.

"You don't know what you're missing. Put a bit of treacle or sugar on it."

"I don't want it," Mary repeated. Instead, she ate some toast with marmalade and drank some tea. Martha then told her to wear warm clothes and run out to play.

"Outside? Why should I go out on a day like this?"

"Well, what will you do in here?"

"Who will go with me?"

Martha stared at her for a minute.

Then she told Mary she'd have to play by herself. She also mentioned that one of the gardens had been locked up for ten years.

"Why?" asked Mary.

"Mr. Craven locked it up after his wife

died suddenly. It was her garden. He dug a hole and buried the key. Oh! That's Mrs. Medlock ringing the bell. I have to go now."

Mary couldn't help thinking about the locked-up garden. She wondered what it looked like.

Eventually, Mary ventured outside. She passed through the shrubbery gate and found herself in a large garden, with wide lawns and winding walks with clipped borders. There were trees, and flower beds, and evergreens clipped into strange shapes, and a large pool with an old gray fountain in the middle. But the flower beds were bare and wintry, and the fountain was not working. This was not the garden that was locked up.

She was just thinking this, when she saw that at the end of the path she was following, there seemed to be a long wall with ivy growing over it. She went toward

The Secret Garden

the wall and found that there was a green door in the ivy, and that it was open. She went through the door and saw a garden with walls all around it and that it was only one of many such ones. She saw another open green door, revealing bushes and pathways between beds containing winter vegetables. Fruit trees were trained flat against the wall, and over some of the beds there were glass frames. A man with a spade walked through a door leading to the second garden. Startled at seeing her, he raised his cap to her. He didn't seem pleased to see her. She felt the same way.

"What is this place?" she asked.

"A kitchen garden," he answered.

"Can I go into it?"

"If you like. But there's nothing to see."

She walked past the second green door and came to a door that was shut. Hoping it was the one that led to the garden, she

was disappointed to see that the door opened easily to an orchard. She looked for the door to the locked-up garden, but to no avail.

She wondered if she'd ever find the key. She wondered why Mr. Craven, who had loved his wife, hated her garden enough to lock it. She saw a robin with a red breast singing in a tree top. She passed it and noticed the tree it was on, and stopped suddenly.

"I believe that tree is in the secret garden; in fact I'm sure it is!"

She walked back to the first kitchen garden and saw the old man digging there. She stood there for a while. He took no notice of her, so she spoke to him.

"I didn't see a door leading to the other garden."

"What garden?" He stopped and looked at her.

"The one on the other side of the wall," said Mary. "I saw the treetops. A bird with a red breast was sitting on one of them and was singing."

On hearing that, the gardener smiled, which surprised Mary. She thought he looked much nicer when he smiled. He whistled softly, and suddenly the robin flew toward him and landed on a soft cloth near his feet.

"There he is," he said, like he was speaking to a child.

"Where have you been, you cheeky beggar? I haven't seen you. Have you started courting already? You're too fast!"

The bird looked very comfortable

around the man. He hopped about and pecked the earth briskly, looking for seeds and insects. It actually gave Mary a strange feeling in her heart, because he was so pretty and cheerful and seemed so like a person. He had a tiny plump body and a delicate beak, and slender, delicate legs.

"Will he always come when you call him?" she asked almost in a whisper.

"Yes, he will. I've known him since he was a baby."

"What bird is he?"

"Don't you know? He's a robin redbreast, and they are the friendliest, most curious birds around. He's always coming to see what I'm planting."

The robin hopped about busily pecking the soil, and now and then stopped and looked up at them. Mary thought his black dew-drop eyes gazed at her with great curiosity. It really seemed as if he was finding out all about her. The strange feeling in her heart increased. "Where did the rest of the brood fly to?" she asked.

"No idea. They are out of their nests before they know it. He's a lonely one."

"I'm lonely, too," she said softly.

The old man pushed back his cap and looked at her. "Are you the one from India?"

She nodded.

"No wonder you're lonely," he said. He continued digging deeply after that.

"What's your name?" she asked.

"Ben Weatherstaff," he replied with a sour chuckle. "I'm lonely myself, except when he's around." He added, nodding toward the robin's direction, "He's the only friend I have."

"I have no friends. I never had any. My ayah didn't like me, and I never played with anyone," Mary said.

"You and me, we're alike. We don't look good, and I bet we got tempers."

Mary never considered the fact that she could actually be ill-tempered or that she could look as bad as Ben. She felt uncomfortable. Suddenly a clear rippling little sound broke out near her and she turned round. She was standing a few feet from a young apple tree and the robin had flown onto one of its branches and had burst out into a scrap of a song. Ben Weatherstaff laughed outright.

"What did he do that for?" asked Mary.

"He's made up his mind to make friends with you," replied Ben. "He took a fancy to you."

"To me?" said Mary, and she moved toward the little tree softly and looked up.

"Would you make friends with me?" she said to the robin just as if she were speaking to a person. "Would you?" And

she did not say it either in her hard
little voice or in her imperious Indian
voice, but in a tone so soft, eager, and
coaxing that Ben Weatherstaff was as
surprised as she had been when she heard
him whistle.

"You talk to him just as Dickon talks
to his animals on the moor."

"Who's Dickon?" she asked.

"He's Martha's brother. He has a way with plants and animals."

She was as curious about Dickon as she was about the secret garden. She was about to ask more questions about him when the robin suddenly ended his song, shook his wings, and flew away.

"Oh, he's flown away! To the tree in the garden with no doors," Mary cried.

"He lives there. It's where he hatched. Lives in a rose tree."

"A rose tree? I would like to see it. Are there more?"

"Look here, don't go poking your nose around here, all right?" he told her sharply. "I have work to do now. Run along and play."

He stopped digging, threw his spade over his shoulder, and walked off without even glancing at her or saying good-bye.

CHAPTER 5

The Cry in the Corridor

At first, each day was like every other. Mary woke up in her room to find Martha building the fire; she ate her breakfast in the nursery; she would gaze out of the window across the moor. Realizing there was nothing indoors for her, she walked out. She ran to make herself warm. She hated the wind that rushed at her face and roared and held her back. But the big breaths of rough fresh air blown over the heather were good for her whole thin body. It whipped some red color into her cheeks and brightened her dull eyes. After a few days she wakened one morning knowing what it was to be hungry, and when she sat down to her breakfast, she took up her spoon and began to eat her porridge until her bowl was empty.

"This is a surprise!" said Martha.

"It tasted good," said Mary, a bit surprised herself.

"It's the air from the moor that's making you have an appetite. Continue

playing outdoors every day and you'll get some flesh on you. You won't be so yellow."

"I don't play outside. I have nothing to play with."

"Nothing to play with?" exclaimed Martha. "Play with whatever nature gives you!"

Mary just took walks and looked around. Sometimes she'd see Ben Weatherstaff gardening, but he looked too sour to talk to. Once he even picked up his spade and walked away on seeing her.

One day, she was looking up at a long spray of ivy swinging in the wind when she saw a gleam of scarlet and heard a brilliant chirp—and there, on the top of the wall, perched Ben Weatherstaff's robin redbreast, tilting forward to look at her.

"Oh! It's you!" she cried. He twittered and chirped and hopped along the wall as if he were telling her all sorts of things. It seemed to Mistress Mary as if she understood him, too, though he was not speaking in words. It was as if he said:

"Good morning! Isn't the sun nice? Isn't everything nice? Let us both chirp and hop and twitter. Come on! Come on!"

Mary began to laugh, and as he hopped and took little flights along the wall she ran after him.

"I like you! I like you!" she cried out, pattering down the walk; and she chirped and tried to whistle. The robin seemed to be quite satisfied and chirped and whistled back at her. At last he spread his wings and made a darting flight to the top of a tree, where he perched and sang loudly. That reminded Mary of the first time she had seen him. He had been swinging on a treetop then, and she had been standing in the orchard. Now she was on the other side of the orchard and standing in the path outside a much lower wall. She noticed the same tree inside the walls.

The Secret Garden

"It's in the secret garden, the one with no door. How I wish I could go in." She looked all around, but found no door leading to that particular garden. She remembered Martha telling her about a door being there ten years ago and that Mr. Craven had buried the key.

This gave her a lot to think about and suddenly she wasn't sorry she had come to Misselthwaite Manor. She'd stay outdoors all day and would only come back for supper after which she'd feel drowsy and comfortable. She even started to like having Martha around and liked hearing her nonstop chatter. One night she asked Martha why Mr. Craven hated the garden.

"It was the garden Mrs. Craven first made when they got married, and she loved it. They tended the flowers together. No other gardener was allowed inside. They'd go in and shut the door and stay there for hours, reading and talking. There was an old tree with a branch bent like a seat. She grew roses around it. But one day, she was sitting on the branch when it broke and she fell. The pain was so unbearable that she died. The doctors thought the master would die of grief himself. That's why he hates the garden now. Nobody has gone in since. He won't allow it."

Four good things had happened to

The Secret Garden

Mary since she had come to Misselthwaite Manor. She had felt as if she had understood a robin and that he had understood her; she had run in the wind until her blood had grown warm; she had been healthily hungry for the first time in her life; and she had found out what it was to be sorry for someone. As she was listening to the wind howl outside, she heard another sound. She didn't know what it was at first, but then she thought it sounded like a child crying, even though it sounded far away.

"Did you hear someone cry?" she asked Martha.

"No," she said, "that's the wind making the noise."

"But it's coming from the house, from one of the corridors," said Mary.

At that moment the door opened with a bang due to a strong gust of wind from outside that made both of them jump.

They heard the cry again clearly now.

"There!" cried Mary. "I told you someone was crying; it wasn't a grown-up."

Martha ran to shut the door and locked it with a key. "It was the wind," she said stubbornly. "If not, it must've been Betty Butterworth, the scullery maid. She's been having a bad toothache all day."

But Mary didn't believe her, not in the troubled and awkward manner in which she spoke.

CHAPTER 6

"There was someone crying—there was!"

Mary couldn't go out the next day, as it was raining heavily. She asked Martha what she did in her cottage when it rained like this.

"The oldest ones go and play in the cowshed. Dickon doesn't mind getting wet; he goes out just the same. Me, I try to keep from getting under each other's feet mostly. Eh, there sure are a lot of us!"

Mary finally stopped resenting Martha's talk. She found it interesting and even felt

63

sorry to hear it stop. The things her ayah had told her were quite different from the things Martha told her. Of all the people Martha spoke about in her family of fourteen, Mary liked the mother, as she liked hearing stories of her, and of Dickon and his pets as well.

"If I had a raven or a fox cub like Dickon has, I could play with it," said Mary. "But I have nothing."

Martha looked surprised. "Can you knit?" she asked.

"No," answered Mary.

"Can you sew?"

"No."

"Can you read?"

"Yes."

"Then why don't you read something? You can improve your spelling. You can start reading the good book at your age."

"I don't have any books. Those I had, I left in India," Mary said.

"Pity, then!" said Martha. "If Mrs. Medlock allows you to go to the library, there are thousands of books there."

Mary liked what she heard and decided to find the library herself. She was not worried about Mrs. Medlock. In this house, the servants lived a luxurious life when the master wasn't there. Mary thought looking for the library would give her a chance to explore the house a bit more. Were there really a hundred rooms? She wondered if they were locked. She thought she'd go and count the number of doors, as there was nothing else to do that morning. Since she didn't know a thing about authority, she didn't think about asking Mrs. Medlock's permission.

When she stepped out into the corridor, she saw that it was a long one that branched out into other corridors, and it even had a flight of stairs. There were many doors and pictures on the wall.

Some were of dark and curious landscapes, but others were mostly of men and women dressed grandly in satins and velvets. She found herself in a gallery full of paintings. She felt the faces stare at her as she walked down. Some were pictures of children—little girls in thick satin frocks that reached to their feet and stood

out about them, and boys with puffed sleeves and lace collars and long hair, or with big ruffles around their necks. She always stopped to look at the children, and wonder what their names were, and where they had gone, and why they wore such odd clothes. There was a stiff, plain little girl rather like herself. She wore a green brocade dress and held a green parrot on her finger. Her eyes had a sharp, curious look.

"Where do you live now?" she thought. "I wish you were here."

It felt odd to walk down the long corridors that seemed to have never been visited. She thought of trying the doors when she came to the second floor. They were all locked, as Mrs. Medlock had said, but when she tried her hand on one of them, she found it open.

She pushed the massive door open and entered a big bedroom. There were embroidered hangings on the wall, and inlaid furniture similar to what she had seen in India stood about the room. A broad window with leaded panes looked out upon the moor; and over the mantel was another portrait of the stiff, plain little girl who seemed to stare at her more curiously than ever. Maybe this was her room, thought Mary.

There were curious pieces of furniture in most of the rooms. In one room, which looked like a lady's sitting room, the hangings were all embroidered velvet, and in a cabinet were about a hundred little elephants made of ivory.

She opened the door of the cabinet and stood on a footstool and played with these for quite a long time. When she got tired, she set the elephants in order and shut the door of the cabinet.

She felt too tired to walk any farther, so she turned back. She lost her way in the long corridors a couple of times. "I believe I have taken a wrong turn again," she said, standing still at what seemed to be the end of a short passage with tapestries on the wall. "I don't know which way

to go."

While she stood there, she heard a sound. It was another cry, not like the last one, but a short, childish whine that was muffled due to the walls.

"It seems closer this time," Mary said. "And it's crying."

She accidently put her hand on the tapestry near her and was startled when it sprang back. The tapestry covered a door that fell open into another corridor. She saw Mrs. Medlock ready to step out, looking very cross.

"What are you doing here?" she demanded. "What have I told you?"

"I turned around a wrong corner, and I heard someone crying," said Mary.

"You'll go to your room this instant, or I'll box your ears!"

She was half dragged into her room.

"Now," said Mrs. Medlock, "you'll stay where you're supposed to or you'll find

yourself locked up. The master should get you a governess, like he said he would. I've got too much to do."

She went out of the room and slammed the door after her, and Mary sat on the

hearth rug, pale with rage.

"There was someone crying—there was—there was!"

She heard the cry twice, and she was sure to find out what it was soon.

CHAPTER 7

The Key to the Garden

Two days later, Mary woke up and called out to Martha to look at the moor. The storm had ended, leaving behind bright blue skies with tiny puffs of clouds.

"I thought it was always dark and gloomy in England," said Mary.

"Not in the least!" snorted Martha.

"Can I come to see your cottage?" asked Mary.

"I'll ask my mum about it. It's my day off, and I'm going home. I am so happy to be going home!"

After giving Mary her breakfast, Martha happily left, knowing that she was going home for the day.

Mary ran around the garden, enjoying the sun on her face. She felt much better now! She went into the first kitchen garden and found Ben Weatherstaff working there with two other gardeners.

She asked him, "Do you think robin remembers me?"

"Of course he does!" cried Ben.

She heard a chirp and a twitter, and when she looked at the bare flower bed, she saw him hopping about, pretending to peck things out of the earth. But she knew he had followed her, and the thought filled her with delight.

"You do remember me!" she cried out. "You do! You are prettier than anything else in the world!" She was so happy that she scarcely dared to breathe.

She saw him hop over a small pile of freshly turned up earth. He stopped on it to look for a worm. The earth had been turned up because a dog had been trying to dig up a mole and he had scratched quite a deep hole.

As Mary looked at the hole curiously, she saw something almost buried in the newly turned soil.

It was something like a ring of rusty iron or brass, and when the robin flew up into a tree nearby, she put out her hand and picked the ring up. It was more than a ring, however; it was an old key that looked as if it had been buried a long time.

"Perhaps it has been buried for ten years," she said in a whisper. "Perhaps it is the key to the garden!"

CHAPTER 8

The Robin Who Showed the Way

She looked at the key for a long time, all the while wondering if this was the key to the secret garden. She wondered if the garden had changed over the last ten years. She thought she could go into the garden every day and shut the door behind her and play, and nobody would ever know where she was. The thought pleased her very much.

Martha returned the next day. She was full of stories of the delights of her day out.

"I told them all about you," Martha continued. "They were very interested in hearing about your life in India."

"I'll tell you a great deal more," Mary said. "I dare say they would like to hear about riding on elephants and camels, and about the officers going to hunt tigers."

That delighted Martha immensely. "Oh, I am sure they would love to hear about it!"

Mary gave her a long, steady look. "You cheer me up, Martha," she said. "I like to hear you talk."

Martha went out of the room and came back with something held in her hands under her apron. "Well, I got you a present!" she said, beaming.

"For me?" cried Mary.

Martha brought it out from under her apron and exhibited it quite proudly.

It was a strong, slender rope with a striped red-and-blue handle at each end, but Mary Lennox had never seen a skipping rope before. She gazed at it with a mystified expression. "What is it for?" she asked curiously.

"You're telling me they've got lions and tigers and elephants in India, but no skipping ropes?"

She then started skipping across the room. Mary got up from her chair, looking excited.

"Do you think I can skip like that?"

"You can try. My mother told me, 'Let her play out in the fresh air skipping an' it'll stretch her legs an' arms an' give her some strength in them.'"

It was plain that there was not a great deal of strength in Mistress Mary's arms and legs when she first began to skip. She was not very good at it, but she liked it so much that she did not want to stop.

"Put your things on and go outdoors," said Martha. Mary put on her coat and hat and took her skipping rope over her arm. She opened the door and left. The skipping rope was a wonderful thing. She counted and skipped, and skipped and counted, until her cheeks were quite red, and she was more interested than she had ever been since she was born. She skipped around the fountain garden and at last into the kitchen garden, where she saw Ben Weatherstaff digging and talking to his robin, which was hopping around him. She skipped down the walk toward him, and he lifted his head and looked at her with a curious expression.

"Well, now, what have we here?" said Ben.

"A skipping rope. I can't skip that well just yet," said Mary. "I've only just started."

Ben pointed at the robin. "He'll want to know all about the skipping rope, for he's never seen one."

Mary skipped around all the gardens and around the orchard, resting every few minutes. The robin had followed her, and he greeted her with a chirp. As Mary skipped toward him, she felt something heavy in her pocket strike against her at each jump. She laughed.

"You showed me where the key was yesterday," she said. "You ought to show me the door today; but I don't believe you know!"

The Secret Garden

Suddenly the gust of wind swung aside some loose ivy trails on the wall, and she saw under it a round knob that had been covered by the leaves hanging over it. It was the knob of a door.

She pushed aside the thick leaves and ivy while her heart began to thump and her hands to shake a little in her delight and excitement.

This was the door to the secret garden! She took out the key from her pocket, put it in the keyhole, and turned it twice. She had to use a bit of effort, but that did it. She took a deep breath and looked around to see if anyone was coming. Seeing that she was all alone, she pushed the door slowly. Then she slipped through it and shut it behind her. She stood with her back against it, looking about her in wonder and delight, breathing hard with excitement.

She was standing inside the secret garden!

CHAPTER 9

A Strange Place to Live In

It was the sweetest, most mysterious-looking place anyone could imagine. All the ground was covered with grass of a wintry brown and out of it grew clumps of bushes that were surely rose bushes if they were alive. It was different from any other place she had ever seen in her life.

"How still it is!" she whispered. She waited and listened to the silence. Even the robin didn't make a sound or flutter his wings.

"I'm the first person to speak here in ten years!" said an astonished Mary.

She moved softly, as if trying not to wake anyone. She was inside the wonderful garden, and she could come through the door under the ivy anytime. She felt as if she had found a world all her own.

The robin flew down from his treetop and hopped about or flew after her from one bush to another. He chirped a good

deal and had a very busy air, as if he were showing her things. Everything was strange and silent, and she seemed to be hundreds of miles away from anyone, but somehow she did not feel lonely at all. She decided to skip across the entire garden. The exercise made her so warm that she first threw her coat off, and then her hat.

After she got back, she looked so pretty with rosy cheeks and bright eyes and she ate her dinner so well that Martha nearly wept with joy. Mary looked at the fire and thought she should be careful if she wanted to keep her secret kingdom.

"This is such a big, empty place," she said slowly, "and the gardens are lonely. I thought if I had a little spade I could dig somewhere and make a little garden if I get some seeds."

Martha looked delighted. "Good idea!"

"I've got money."

"I just thought of something!" said Martha. "We can give a letter to Dickon to go to the village and get the spade and seeds."

"Oh, that's kind of you! I'll surely write the letter," Mary exclaimed.

"I've got pen, paper, and ink!" Martha cried, and ran out to get it. When Martha returned, they sat down and wrote a letter to Dickon.

"We'll put the money in the envelope and send it with the butcher boy. He's good friends with Dickon," said Martha.

"I'll finally get to meet him?" asked Mary with happiness.

"Yes," said Martha, a bit surprised at her reaction.

Martha stayed with her until teatime, and just before Martha went downstairs for the tea tray, Mary asked a question.

"Martha," she said, "has the scullery maid had the toothache again today?"

Martha looked startled for a bit. "Why do you ask?"

"I heard that far-off crying today again, just like the other night. It couldn't have been the wind, for there is none blowing."

"You mustn't go down corridors listening," said Martha. "Mr. Craven would get angry if he knew!"

"I wasn't listening," said Mary. "I was just waiting for you—and I heard it."

"Oh! That's Mrs. Medlock's bell. I have to rush!" Martha said, and she ran out of the room without looking back.

"What a strange house," said Mary drowsily. The moment she put her head on the pillow, she fell asleep.

CHAPTER 10

Dickon

For a week the sun shone on the secret garden. That was the name Mary gave it. It was like a fairy garden. Mary liked being outdoors. She loved the wind, and she could run faster now and could skip to a hundred. Mary worked and dug and pulled out weeds with determination in the garden day after day, becoming more and more pleased with her work. She often wondered how long it would be before the flowers started growing. She became closer to Ben Weatherstaff. He didn't even object to her watching him while he worked. One morning, he stood up from work and looked at her.

"How long have you been here?" he asked.

"A month, I think," Mary replied. "What would you plant if you had a garden of your own?"

"Bulbs and roses," Ben answered.

Mary's face lit up. "You like roses?"

Ben nodded.

"Do they die? Do roses die if they're left by themselves?" she asked.

"If the soil isn't good enough. But why do you care about roses all of a sudden?" he demanded.

Mary felt her face go red. She was a little afraid to answer.

"I-I have nothing else to do," she stammered softly.

When she reached a little gate, she heard a whistling sound. She turned and saw a boy sitting under a tree.

He was playing a rough wooden pipe. He was about twelve, with an upturned nose, rosy cheeks, and big blue eyes. He looked very clean. When he saw Mary, he began to rise from the ground.

"I'm Dickon," he said, "and I know you're Miss Mary."

He spoke to her like he knew her well. So she asked him if he got Martha's letter. He nodded his curly, rust-colored head. "That's why I'm here."

He bent to pick up something that was on the ground. "I got your tools. There's a spade, a rake, a fork, and a hoe. There's a trowel, too. I have some good seeds here, too."

"Will you show me how to plant them?" she asked.

Just then he looked around. "Where is that robin calling us to?"

"Is it really calling us?" asked Mary.

"Sure! It calls out to anyone it's friends with."

Mary turned to look at him. "Can you keep a secret? I have a big one. I believe I'd die if anyone found out!" she said fiercely.

Though puzzled, he replied, "Aye, I'm

good with secrets."

"I've stolen a garden. It isn't mine or anybody else's. Nobody cares for it and I don't know what to do," she whispered.

"Where is it?" asked Dickon in a dropped voice.

Mary got up and said, "Come with me and I'll show you."

When she stepped to the wall

and lifted the hanging ivy, he gasped. There was a door, and Mary pushed it slowly open. They passed in together, and then Mary stood and waved her hand around defiantly.

"It's this," she said. "It's a secret garden, and I'm the only one in the world who wants it to be alive."

Dickon looked around and exclaimed, "Whoa! It's like walking into a dream!"

CHAPTER 11

Inside the Secret Garden

"I never thought I'd see this place," he whispered.

"Did you know about it?" she asked.

Since she was speaking loudly, he motioned for her to keep quiet, telling her that they must talk softly. He then said that he knew about the garden. "Martha told me about it."

They went around the garden, Dickon showing her that most of the plants were still alive somehow. How thrilled Mary was to know that! They went from bush to bush and from tree to tree. He was very strong and clever with his knife and knew how to cut the dry and dead wood away, and he could tell when an unpromising bough or twig still had green life in it. In the course of half an hour Mary thought she could tell, too, and when he cut through a lifeless-looking branch, she would cry out joyfully under her breath when she caught sight of the least shade of moist green. The tools came in handy, and she used them like Dickon showed her. Suddenly he saw something that surprised him completely.

"Who did that there?" he asked.

It was Mary's little garden that she had planted by herself. "I did," she answered.

"I thought you didn't know anything about gardening," he told her.

"I don't," she answered, "but they were so little, and the grass was so thick and strong, and they looked as if they had no room to breathe. So I made a place for them."

The Secret Garden

"You're right," he said. "Now they can grow tall and strong, like Jack's beanstalk. There's a lot of work to do here!" he said, looking about excitedly.

"Will you come again and help me

to do it?" Mary begged. "I'm sure I can help, too. I can dig and pull up weeds, and do whatever you tell me. Oh! Do come, Dickon!"

"I'll come because you want me to. I'll come here, be rain or sunshine," he promised. Then he smiled broadly. "We'll have so much fun!"

He looked around now with a thoughtful expression on his face. "It does look like a secret garden, but it also feels like someone has been here in the last ten years."

"But the door was locked. No one could get in," argued Mary.

"It looks like someone's done some pruning over the last few years. But how? With the door locked and key buried?"

She then leaned forward and asked him something she hadn't asked anyone else. "Do you like me?"

The Secret Garden

"Aye! I do like you, very much, as much as the robin!"

"Same goes for me!" said Mary. They started working joyfully, and Mary was so upset when it was time for the midday meal. "I have to go for my meal."

"Me, I've got my meal with me," said Dickon.

Mary was halfway out of the door when she turned around and asked him, "You won't tell anyone?"

He smiled and promised that he wouldn't, and Mary believed him.

CHAPTER 12

"Might I have a bit of earth?"

Martha was waiting for Mary when she entered her room. "Where have you been? It's quite late."

"I was with Dickon. I finally met him!"

"Dickon? Oh, how did you like him?" asked Martha.

"I think he's wonderful," said Mary with a firm nod, and Martha was surprised to hear that.

After her meal, Mary was about to get her hat when Martha stopped her.

"I want to tell you something. Mr. Craven has come back and I think he wants to see you."

"What for? He didn't want to see me when I came," cried Mary.

"My mother met him in the village and said something about you that made him want to meet you. He'll do so before he leaves again. He'll be gone till autumn or winter this time."

"Oh! That's wonderful!" Mary shouted, for if Mr. Craven wasn't going to be there for all these months, she could look after the garden better. Just then, Mrs. Medlock entered the room and looked at Mary.

"Her hair is rough, Martha. Brush it and put a nice dress on her. Mr. Craven wants to meet her in his study."

All the pink left Mary's cheeks. She stood absolutely silent while she was readied by Martha. She was taken to a part of the house she had not been to before. At last Mrs. Medlock knocked at a door, and when someone said, "Come in," they entered the room together.

A man was sitting in an armchair before the fire, and Mrs. Medlock spoke to him.

"This is Miss Mary, sir," she said.

"You can go and leave her here. I will ring for you when I want you to take her away," said Mr. Craven. After she left, he told Mary to come closer.

"Are you well?" he asked.

"Yes," answered Mary.

"Do they take good care of you?"

"Yes."

"I forgot you," he said. "I intended to send you a governess or a nurse, but I forgot."

"Please, sir, don't get me a governess! I'm too old for one," begged Mary.

"All right, if that's what you want."

"I'd like something else, too, sir, if you don't mind."

"What?" asked Mr. Craven.

"Might I have a bit of earth?" she asked. For a moment he just looked at her as though she had reminded him of something. His eyes grew soft and warm.

"Of course, from anywhere you like. Now go, I'm tired." He rang the bell for Mrs. Medlock. "Good-bye. I'll be away all summer."

The Secret Garden

When Mrs. Medlock left her at the end of her own corridor, Mary flew back to her room. She found Martha waiting there. Martha had, in fact, hurried back after she had removed the dinner service.

"I can have my garden!" cried Mary. "I may have it where I like! And I am not going to have a governess for a long time!"

"Isn't that nice of him?" said a delighted Martha.

"He really is a nice man, and he looks so miserable!"

She ran back to the garden to tell Dickon the good news, but found no one there. Suddenly, she saw a picture stuck to a tree with a thorn, and on it was written: "I will come back."

CHAPTER 13

"I am Colin"

Mary knew that the message meant that he would keep her secret safe. She liked Dickon even more now!

Early the next morning, it was raining quite heavily. Mary looked at the storm outside with anger and disappointment, for she thought it was raining because she didn't wish for it to. She had been lying awake turning from side to side for about an hour when suddenly she turned to the door and listened.

The door of her room was ajar, and

the sound came from down the corridor, a far-off faint sound of fretful crying. She listened for a few minutes, and each minute she became even surer.

"I am going to find out what it is," she said. "Everybody is in bed, and I don't care about Mrs. Medlock—I don't care!"

She took a candle and walked down the corridor to the tapestry. She knew that it really was a door.

She pushed it open very gently and

closed it behind her, and she stood in the corridor and could hear the crying quite plainly, though it was not loud. It was on the other side of the wall to her left, and a few yards farther there was a door. So she walked to the door and into a very handsomely furnished room. And there, on the bed, was a boy crying!

Mary thought she was dreaming. The boy had a sharp, delicate face the color of ivory, and eyes too big for it. He had also a lot of hair, which tumbled over his forehead in heavy locks and made his thin face seem smaller. He looked like a boy who had been ill, but he was crying more as if he were tired and cross than as if he were in pain.

He opened his eyes and saw her. "Are you a ghost?" he said at last in a half-frightened whisper.

"No, I'm not," Mary answered, her own whisper sounding half frightened.

The Secret Garden

"Are you?"

He stared at her. "No," he replied after waiting a moment or so. "I'm Colin Craven. Who are you?"

"I'm Mary Lennox. Mr. Craven is my uncle."

"He is my father," said the boy.

"Your father!" gasped Mary. "No one ever told me he had a son!"

"Come here," he said.

When she did, he put his hand on hers. "You are real. I thought I was dreaming."

"You aren't. Didn't anyone tell you I was coming?"

He shook his head.

"Why?"

"Because I'm always ill and I have to lie down. My father won't let me talk to anyone. He doesn't want to see me, either."

Mary asked why. He told her that it was because he reminded his father of his dead mother.

"He hates the garden because she died," mumbled Mary.

"What garden?" Colin asked.

"A garden she used to like." She fumbled. "Have you always been here?"

"Almost. He told them to keep me out in the fresh air. I hate fresh air and I don't want to go out."

"If you don't like people to see you," she began, "do you want me to leave?"

"No. I want to know more about you. Talk to me." Mary put down her candle on the table near the bed and sat down on the cushioned stool.

"What do you want me to tell you?" she asked. She answered all his questions about where she came from, how long had she been living at Misselthwaite Manor. She learned that even though he was an invalid, he was given everything a child could wish for.

"Everyone has to do as I please," he

said angrily. "No one believes I'll live. How old are you?" he asked.

"I am ten," answered Mary, forgetting herself for a moment, "and so are you."

"How do you know that?" he demanded in a surprised voice.

"Because when you were born, the garden door was locked and the key was buried. And it has been locked for ten years."

Colin sat up, interested. "Why is the garden locked? Where's the key?"

"Mr. Craven locked it. He buried the key," she replied nervously. "Do you think you won't live?" she asked, in the hope of making him forget the garden.

"I don't suppose I shall," he answered as indifferently as he had spoken before.

"I have heard you crying three times," Mary said, "but I did not know who it was. Were you crying about that?" She wanted him to forget the garden.

"Talk about the garden. Don't you want to see it? I surely do! I will make them take me there!"

"Don't! Then it won't be a secret anymore!" cried Mary.

"Secret? What do you mean?"

"No one knows about it but us!" After a while she said, "Perhaps we could go alone and it would always be a secret garden?"

"I should—like—that," he said very slowly, his eyes looking dreamy. "I should like that. I should not mind fresh air in a secret garden. If you stay in a room, you never see things. You know a lot of things. I feel as if you had been inside that garden."

After a moment he said, "I'm going to show you something." He showed her a portrait of his mother. "I don't know why she died. I hate her at times for it." A moment of uncomfortable silence passed.

"What would Mrs. Medlock do if she found out that I had been here?" Mary inquired, trying to divert his mind.

"She would do as I told her to do," he answered.

"Do you know Martha? She waits on me," Mary said at his nod. She suddenly understood why Martha acted strange on hearing the "noise." "Martha knew about you all the time?" she asked.

"Yes. She often attends to me. The nurse likes to get away from me, and then Martha comes."

"I should go. You look sleepy." She stayed with him till he fell asleep.

CHAPTER 14

The Young Rajah

In the morning, Mary told Martha that she knew about Colin. Martha's face became pale with fear.

"Oh, God! You'll get me into trouble for this. I've not told you a word of him, yet I'll get the boot! How come I didn't hear him screaming at you?" asked Martha.

"He wasn't angry. He was happy to see me. We talked for a long time."

"Really?" said Martha, calming down a bit. "You must've impressed him. The boy's a terror when even the slightest thing is out of place. He doesn't see strangers. What if

119

he tells Mrs. Medlock? She'll have me out of here!"

"He'll see that it doesn't happen. Everyone does as he pleases, right?"

"Aye, that's true."

"He's a nice boy, Martha. What's wrong with him?"

"I'm not sure. Mr. Craven went mad when his wife died. He thought Colin would be a hunchback like him, so he kept him from his sight and in bed all the time. Colin has fevers, chest colds, and flus that make him sleep like the dead."

"Is he dying?" asked Mary.

"No idea. Mother says a child who doesn't breathe fresh air or who stays in a dark room for a long time doesn't grow well. Considering all that, plus seeing Mrs. Medlock's face when he wakes up, he must wish himself dead."

"We should take him outside more. It did me good," suggested Mary.

"Last time we took him out, he had such a fit, he got a high fever!" Just then, Martha ran to answer a bell that rang in the hall. She looked dazed when she returned.

"He's asked for you. The boy was sitting and reading and was asking for you!"

Martha took Mary to Colin's room. He was wearing a red robe, and his room was well lit.

"Mary, I have been thinking about you all morning!"

"Me too. Colin, can you tell Martha that you won't let Mrs. Medlock fire her when she finds out about this?"

"Nobody will do a thing I don't want! Send her in." Colin proceeded to tell Martha that her fears were baseless and that he would take care of her. After she left, he asked Mary, "What are you thinking?"

"I'm thinking of how you reminded

The Secret Garden

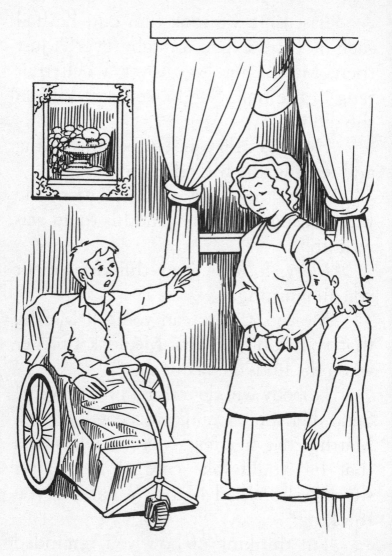

me of an Indian rajah just now! The way you spoke to Martha was exactly like that. I was also thinking of how different you are from Dickon."

"Who's Dickon?"

Mary told him all about Dickon, who was lively, smart, and good with nature.

"How can he like the moor?" wondered Colin.

"Oh, it's the most gorgeous place! Many flowers and animals live there," Mary cried.

"You don't see a thing when you're ill," grumbled Colin. "I can't even go out! I'm going to die!"

At that moment, Mary felt no pity for the boy. She put her hands on her waist and narrowed her eyes. "You say it because others say it. Let's not talk about death anymore."

They didn't. They poured their hearts out to each other. She spoke like she had never done, and he spoke and listened more than he had in his life! They laughed at silly things like normal children did— not like a hard, rude girl and a frail boy who thought he was going to die. Just then Mrs. Medlock entered with Dr. Craven, who was the boy's uncle and doctor. Both of them were quite startled!

"Good Lord! What's this?" cried Mrs. Medlock.

"She's my cousin, Mary Lennox," Colin said after the doctor threw an angry look at both him and Mrs. Medlock. "I like her and I want her to come see me when I want."

Dr. Craven turned on Mrs. Medlock, who started stuttering, "Sir! I don't know how it happened! The servants had their orders and—"

"She found me on her own," Colin interrupted. "She heard me crying last night and found me." Though neither of them looked pleased, the doctor

and Mrs. Medlock didn't voice their objections. The doctor checked his pulse. "Too much excitement, boy. Not good at all."

"It definitely won't be good if she is

kept away. Ask the maids to bring tea and snacks. We'll have it here," said Colin.

The doctor reminded him that he was not to forget that he was quite ill.

"I want to forget it," pleaded Colin. "She helps me! That's why I want her."

Dr. Craven walked to the door and turned around one last time. He thought how much better the boy did look—all because of that girl's presence! Sighing, he left.

"So," said Colin as he grabbed a hot muffin, "tell me again about the rajahs."

CHAPTER 15

After the Rains

Because of the heavy rains that continued over the next week, Mary didn't have a chance to meet Dickon or go to the garden. She spent hours with Colin talking about Dickon, the gardens, the moor, India. They would go through his picture books and read to each other. Mary was very careful not to talk about the secret garden too much. It had been hers for a short time and she wanted to share it with no one except Dickon. She needed to trust Colin first. She had already told him about the garden. Soon she and Dickon could take him out into the garden, and into sunlight and fresh air! She knew it would be good for him, as it had been for her.

The first morning the sun came through the window and fell on Mary's face, she woke up with a jolt and thought of the garden. She could go there today and see how it had fared! She dressed herself and ran out the door. She ran out of the house and down the paths leading to the secret garden. She raced along the ivy-curtained wall, toward the hidden door.

Just then she heard the loud CAW of a crow. It gave her a fright as it spread its wings and flew inside the garden. Hoping he wouldn't stay, she entered the garden. There she saw Dickon, shovel in hand, working on a flower bed. Mary ran to him without a thought.

"Dickon! What are you doing here so early? The sun's hardly up!"

He laughed happily. "I couldn't sleep! Not when the world's begun again! It's working, humming, scratching. Piping and nest building! Look, everything is so different now!"

He was right. Everything had different shades of green in place of gray and brown. Mary clasped her hands and panted like she'd been running for a long time.

"Oh, Dickon! I'm so happy, I can hardly breathe!"

Just then, a little bushy-tailed animal came out from under a tree, and the crow flew and perched on Dickon's shoulder.

"Some friends of mine from the moor have come with me. The little fox cub is Captain and the crow here is Soot." Just then Dickon went down on his knees.

"Mary, look at this!"

Mary knelt beside him and saw a large clump of crocuses had burst into purple,

The Secret Garden

orange, and gold. Mary gathered them in her arms and planted kisses on them.

There was every joy in the secret garden that morning. Dickon and Mary walked around the garden, clearing twigs and roots broken by the rains. By the time they were done, it was almost noon. They sat down and Mary told him softly, "There is something I want to tell you."

"What is it?"

"Well, do you know about Colin?"

"What do you know about him?"

"I've seen him. I have been to talk to him every day this week. He wants me to come. He says I make him forget about being ill and dying."

Dickon looked relieved as soon as the surprise died away from his round face.

"That's nice," said Dickon. "I'm glad you found out. Now I don't have to hide it from you. I've never met him, but I've heard that he's got his mother's eyes. That's why his father doesn't see him. He can't bear to look into those eyes."

"Do you think he wants to die?" asked Mary.

"No. I think he wishes he'd never been born. Mother says that's the worst thing for a child, to not feel wanted."

Mary thought about how much those words had been true in her own life. Dickon began playing around with Captain. "You know, if Colin spent more time watching the buds break than waiting for lumps to grow on his back, he'd be a lot healthier!" remarked Dickon.

"I was thinking the exact thing. Each time I talk to him, I think so. I've wondered if he could keep the secret of the garden if we brought him here."

CHAPTER 16

Tantrums

Martha met Mary in the nursery. Mary glowed after all the exercise in the garden and was in a good mood. Martha said, "It's been a bad day with Colin! Why weren't you with him today?"

"I was playing outside with Dickon. What happened?"

"He was in such a terrible mood because you didn't come today. He was whining all the time!" Hearing this, Mary got annoyed. She wouldn't let a spoiled boy ruin things for her. She decided to tell him off. She marched straight to his

133

room, as his crying became more and more hysterical.

"Stop crying!" she yelled. "Stop it this instant! If you scream, I'll scream louder and I'll scare everyone!" she cried, stamping her feet with each sentence. "Why are you still in bed?"

"Why didn't you come see me today?"

"I was outside with Dickon, his fox, and his crow in the sunshine."

"If you meet him instead of coming here, I won't let that boy come here!"

"If you send him away, I'll never come here!" she yelled.

"You selfish girl," he snarled.

"And you're the most selfish boy ever! Not like Dickon. He's the nicest boy alive. What would you know about being nice?"

"I've got a lump on my back. I'm dying!" he cried.

"You aren't!" she said sharply. "You're too nasty to die!"

Rage made Colin sit up straight. He pointed a finger at her. "Get out!" he yelled.

"I'm not ever coming back!" she shouted, and left. She was fuming all the way back to her room. To think she'd almost shared her most precious secret with that beast! She had her dinner alone and crawled into bed. In the night, she heard an extremely loud shriek. She jumped awake. She heard doors slamming and footsteps running down the corridor. Just then, Colin's night nurse, Olivia, burst into her room.

"Thank God you're awake!" she cried.

"Who can sleep with that awful racket?" said Mary. After another cry tore through the house, Mary jumped from the bed and ran to Colin's room.

"STOP THIS INSTANT!" she yelled at the top of her voice. "I hate you! We all do! We should just run out of this house and leave you alone screaming!"

He gasped, too shocked to scream. "But I'm sick!"

"No, you're not," argued Mary.

"But I felt the lump on my back! It'll grow bigger and then I'll die!" He began crying again.

"There is nothing wrong with your back. Nurse, show me his back right now!" she demanded.

She saw that his back was so bony, the spinal cord poked out. "The only lump you felt was that of the bones on your

back! The reason you can feel it is because you're so thin! It's your imagination that's making you behave like this."

As he struggled for deep breaths, he realized she was telling the truth. He looked at his nurse. "I'm going to live?"

"Yes, Colin," said the nurse, "if you don't waste your energy on tantrums and go outside more."

Mary told the nurse to leave. After she left, Colin said, "I'll go into the garden with you if Dickon pushes my chair. I'd like to see his pet fox and crow. Mary, can you tell me about the garden again?"

"Of course, Colin. Just close your eyes." She went on to describe the garden, the soft tone of her voice putting him to sleep.

CHAPTER 17

"You mustn't waste time!"

Mary slept later than usual. She was very tired after all. Colin had a fever, like he always did when he cried a lot. As she ate quietly, Martha told her that he wanted to see her.

"The boy sure likes you! You gave it to him last night, didn't you? Nobody else would've dared!"

After breakfast, Mary went to him. His face looked paler than usual. "I'm glad you've come. My head hurts!" he complained. "Are you going outside?"

"I won't be long," said Mary, leaning against the bedpost. "I have to go to see Dickon about the garden."

"I dreamed of the garden last night!" Colin said with a dreamy smile. "There were green vines and butterflies, and so many birds in their nests! I'll think about it till you return."

Mary joined Dickon in the garden. Soot and Captain were there, too, along with two squirrels that Dickon named Nut and Shell. She told him about all that had happened last night. There was pity on his face.

"Mary, listen to the birds singing. The light, the fresh air, the flowers blooming. We've got to get Colin here. It'll do him good! We mustn't waste time."

"I've got an idea," said Mary. "He wants to meet Soot and Captain. I'll ask him if you can bring them to him. Then, when it's warmer outside, we'll

The Secret Garden

bring him here."

She went back to the house and straight to Colin's room. Her face was glowing, and her hair was ruffled. Colin took a deep breath and smiled. "You smell of flowers!"

"It's the moor you smell on me!" grinned Mary. She told him about the garden blossoming beautifully. She even told him about Dickon, Captain, Soot, Nut, and Shell. She mentioned the sturdy white pony Dickon rode. Dickon had made the pony kiss her cheek with its muzzle.

"Does he understand everything Dickon says?" wondered Colin.

"Apparently," replied Mary. "Dickon says that anything can understand if you're friends with it."

Colin's face fell. "I've never had any creatures as friends. I don't like people, either," he muttered.

"Do you like me?" asked Mary.

"I do!" replied Colin.

He reached out and touched her hand. "Maybe Dickon really is an angel. I shouldn't have said things about sending him away. I'd like to meet him."

"Really?" asked Mary, "Because— because—"

"What is it?" asked Colin.

After a moment she caught his hands

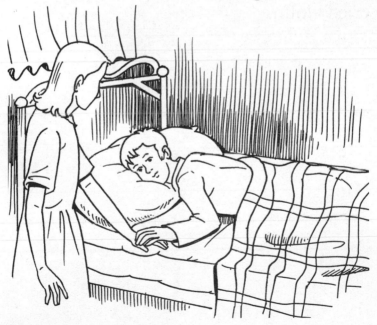

and looked nervously at him. "Can you keep a secret?"

"Yes! Tell me!"

She took a deep breath and said, "I've found the door to the garden. It's under the ivy on the wall. Dickon will meet you tomorrow and then one day you can see the garden yourself!"

"Oh, Mary! That's wonderful!" cried Colin.

CHAPTER 18

It Has Come

Dr. Craven was stunned when he saw Colin laughing and talking with Mary.

Mrs. Medlock looked at them. "She really is good for him," she remarked.

"Doctor! I'm going out in a day or two. I feel better now!" Colin said.

"Don't strain yourself, Colin," warned the doctor.

"I'll go with Mary and Dickon. There's no need for the nurse to come with us."

The doctor laughed. "Well, if you're with Dickon then I've no reason to

worry. Just take it easy!" Saying this,
he left.

Colin ate and slept well that night.
He woke up the next morning in a good

mood and hungry for breakfast. Mary ran in, and Colin could smell the moor and flowers on her.

"You went outside already?" he asked.

"Colin! It has come! Spring has come!" she cried. She went on to describe with passion all that she had seen in the secret garden.

"Mary, open the window! Let some of the fresh air come in."

When the air blew on his face, he took three deep gulps of it. As he continued breathing it, Mary told him about the baby lamb that Dickon had found. He brought it to the garden, where it bonded with the other animals. "He's coming here today," said Mary.

"Nurse!" Colin called imperiously. "I'll be having a fox, a crow, two squirrels, and a lamb visiting me today with Dickon. Make sure they are sent here when they arrive."

The nurse gasped a bit. "Yes, sir."

As they were finishing breakfast, Mary looked about. "Did you hear a moan?"

Colin said, "No, but I think I heard a crow!" Just then Soot flew through the window and Mary opened the door to let Dickon and his furry friends in. Captain walked beside him while he carried the lamb in his hands. Nut stood on one shoulder while Shell poked its head out of his shirt pocket. Colin was overwhelmed looking at this. Dickon walked over, introduced himself, and put the lamb on Colin's lap. The lamb began to nuzzle Colin's robes.

"Hungry little fellow, he is," laughed Dickon as he took out a half-filled baby bottle.

The lamb began to suckle it earnestly. Colin was too touched to say anything,

but Dickon went right on to tell him how he had found the lamb.

"I was on the moor when I heard a weak moan from behind the bushes. I knew it was a newborn lamb. I couldn't find its mother. The lamb on your lap was so weak, it couldn't even move. I found the mother lying dead a little ways away. I took it home, where my mother gave it warm milk and we put it on the rug by the fire."

"Is it getting stronger?" asked Colin.

"Yes! He'll be running about in no time. Fresh milk and fresh air is what he needs."

"Mary says you have a pony, too! Did you ride it here?"

"I did. Oh, you should see what a day it is!" Dickon told him about his ride to the manor. The children spent the next few hours talking and laughing and playing with the animals.

CHAPTER 19

Colin in the Garden

They had to wait a week before Colin could go outdoors, because Colin had a cold and it had gotten chilly. Dickon visited every day, and the three children planned their visit to the garden for hours. They plotted courses and strategies of getting Colin past, unseen.

For Colin, the garden's secrecy was its greatest mystery. He was just as dedicated to keeping the secret as Mary was.

Finally, one morning, when Colin had recovered from his cold, he asked Mrs. Medlock to call the head gardener,

Mr. Roach. The man was very curious, for he had never met the boy; he only knew about his illness and tantrums. He had also heard about the effect the girl from India was having on him.

"Times are changing," said Mrs. Medlock. "Here we are." She turned the doorknob and entered. "Mind the animals you'll see running about."

When Mr. Roach entered the room, he found Colin looking healthy! He was sitting with a delicate girl and a red-haired boy. Animals were running all over the place. Colin was reading to the others.

"Mr. Roach," said Colin in a strong voice, "I'll be going out today and I don't want to be watched. Keep the gardeners off the lawns for this afternoon, please."

After Colin was wrapped in a thick jacket, his servant carried him and his chair to the front door. Dickon held the handles of the wheelchair and steered it onto the lawn. The grounds were empty. They moved slowly with excitement and looked at each plant and grass. They showed him where Ben worked and where the robin sat. At last they came to the ivy wall.

"There's no door here! How did you get in?" cried Colin.

"I wondered about that, too!" laughed Mary. "But look closely."

She lifted the ivy curtain to reveal the door. She unlocked it and opened it. Colin covered his eyes until they were inside.

He slowly opened them and just stared and stared. Mary and Dickon watched him, for he looked different—pink and glowing.

After moments of silence, Colin said with determination, "I will get better! I shall live forever!" Mary agreed.

They pushed the chair under a plum tree with blossoms on it. While the two gardeners worked, Colin sat and watched. He took in each and every detail of the garden. He wondered if he would see the robin. Dickon assured him he would, and took out his pipe to play.

Just then Colin pointed to a tree. "That looks very old. It looks dead."

Mary and Dickon looked at each other. "The roses will bloom and cover the lifelessness with their lovely petals—"

"But it looks like a huge branch has broken," said Colin.

Mary's heart ached, for she knew his mother had died falling off that branch. Suddenly the robin flew and landed at Colin's feet, whistling curiously and looking at the new boy. It flew off just as quickly.

As they worked, Mary was convinced it was magic that had made Colin different today. He appeared healthy with a rosy glow on his face, instead of

The Secret Garden

looking like an ivory statue. Colin said he would come back every afternoon, for he loved the place.

He looked up and saw someone peering over the wall. "Who's that?" he cried.

Mary and Dickon jumped up and glanced to where Colin was pointing. Ben Weatherstaff glared at the children from the ladder in the orchard.

"You should be punished, girl!" he cried. "What are you doing in a place that's prohibited to you? How did you even get in here?" He shook a fist in her direction.

He stopped when he noticed Colin glaring back at him from the wheelchair. Ben's jaw dropped.

"Do you know who I am?" he called. "I'm Colin Craven. You work for my father."

"So you're the cripple!" said Ben.

"I'm not a cripple!" shouted Colin

with murder in his eyes.

"He isn't!" cried Mary. "He's as healthy as I am!"

"So you don't have a crooked back or crooked legs?" asked Ben, for he'd heard many stories.

This was too much for Colin to bear. He threw aside the blanket as Dickon ran to him. He held onto Dickon and stood up.

"There! Do I look like a cripple to you?" he shouted. He looked at Dickon. "I'm standing!" he whispered.

"I knew you could," smiled Dickon. Colin told Mary to bring Ben inside the garden. When he came in, there were tears down his chin. He went to the child.

"Where do you work?" asked Colin.

"Anywhere I'm told," replied Ben. "I'm only here because your mother liked me."

"This was her garden, wasn't it?" asked Colin. Ben nodded.

"It's our garden now. I want it to be

The Secret Garden

a secret. Only my friends and I can come here and you, to help us garden. No one else is to enter!"

"I've tended the garden before. No one knows this! But then my arthritis got bad. Your mother told me to look after the garden if anything happened to her."

On the grass near the tree, Mary had dropped her trowel. Colin stretched out his hand and took it up. An odd expression came onto his face, and he began to scratch at the earth. His thin hand was weak enough, but presently as they watched him—Mary with quite breathless interest—he drove the end of the trowel into the soil and turned some over.

"You can do it!" Mary said to herself.

Colin persevered. After he had turned a few trowelfuls of soil, he spoke exultantly to Dickon in his best Yorkshire.

Ben looked at Colin. "Would you

like me to plant something? A rose, Master Colin?"

"Oh yes! I'd love that!"

Forgetting his arthritis, Ben ran out and came back with his tools and a young plant. He told Colin to plant the rose.

The thin white hands shook a little, and Colin's flush grew deeper as he set the rose in the hole and held it while Ben made the earth firm.

"It's planted!" said Colin at last. "And the sun is setting. Help me up, please, Dickon. I want to be standing when it goes down. That's part of the magic."

Colin planted his first plant and was standing on his own two feet—laughing.

CHAPTER 20

Magic

D r. Craven was waiting when they got back. He started telling Colin not to go out and exert himself. Colin shot back, saying it would be unwise to stop him now.

"You're very rude," grumbled Mary after the doctor sulked out. "You boss people around terribly!" She continued, even at Colin's look of surprise: "You don't know how to be nice to someone. That's why you don't get along with people."

"I don't want to be mean!" protested Colin.

"I was rude and mean when I came here. But I've changed ever since I found the garden!" said Mary.

"That place has magic in it. I just know it!" said Colin.

That is what they truly believed in the months that followed, radiant months of happy, bright days. The garden became lovelier than they had imagined. Green shoots pushed through the earth and over brick walls. They budded, then blossomed into every color and shape. The seeds Mary and Dickon planted grew beautifully. And the roses! They entwined themselves around the tree trunks and bloomed gloriously.

Each flower sent out beautiful fragrances to make a soul happy. It was magic indeed.

One day, Colin wanted to conduct a scientific experiment. So he gathered Mary, Dickon, and Ben and told them:

The Secret Garden

"I believe there is magic in the world. I don't think anyone knows how to make it. I want to test it, if you'll help me.

"The magic here has made me stand today. It's making the changes in the garden. It's making me strong inside! Every day I'll tell myself aloud that there's magic in me and it's making me better! Will you do it with me?" he asked.

All three shouted "Yes!" at once. "Let's start now!" Mary cried and jumped to her feet.

"Sit on the grass," said Colin. "Shall we sway back and forth?"

"No, I can't," said Ben. "I've got the arthritis."

"We'll wait till the magic has taken the stiffness away," Colin said, and at that moment Mary realized how beautiful Colin looked, with his head high like a priest and the light falling on him.

"Let us chant! Close your eyes."

In a melodious voice he began, "The magic is in me! The magic is in Mary! The magic is in Dickon! The magic is in Ben! The magic is in all of us! "

Ben actually began feeling calmer, forgetting the stiffness in his back and knees. Colin stopped chanting and opened his eyes. "Let's take a walk. I'm feeling strong enough."

Leaning against Dickon's strong arm, Colin walked slowly, followed by Ben and Mary and the animals. They covered the entire garden twice. When Colin sat down again, his eyes were filled with tears. "The experiment was successful!"

Ben told him that he'd be up and boxing in no time! Colin looked at him. "Don't be disrespectful. I shan't be a fighter. I'll be a discoverer." Ben was happy that the boy was gaining strength and spirit.

CHAPTER 21

Let Them Laugh

When Dickon didn't work in the garden, he was busy planting or tending vegetables for his mother in the garden around the cottage on the moor. She often sat with him and watched him work. It was their special time.

During one of these times he told her about his friends at the manor and of the secret garden. He spoke of Mary, Colin, and Ben. She was happy to know the garden was doing something good for them all.

"Mary's coming to the manor saved them both!" said Mrs. Sowerby. "What

do the others think of the change in Colin?"

"Mr. Craven hasn't been home in months, but the doctor and the servants are surprised! Colin's even faking his illness a bit so that the doctor won't tell his father. He wants to show him he's healing himself. It's just that Mary and Colin can barely keep from laughing, and they're always hungry!" Dickon chuckled.

Mrs. Sowerby laughed gaily. "Tell you what, lad," she said. "Every morning I'll put a fresh pail of milk along with some nice hot muffins. That way, the hunger can stay away."

"You amaze me, Mother!" said Dickon. "You always know how to make things better for any living creature."

She in turn told him that she was sure they were enjoying themselves. And she was right!

When Dickon brought them fresh milk and muffins, they squealed in delight. But after a week, Colin and Mary realized that this was draining the Sowerby household's finances. So with Mrs. Sowerby's permission, they sent a few shillings back with Dickon to repay her for her kindness.

The Secret Garden

The magic in the garden did wonders for Colin and Mary.

Colin grew stronger every day while Mary grew healthier. Her hair was thick and bouncy now. Everyone in the manor noticed and talked about these changes.

Dr. Craven commented on Colin's change in appetite.

"My appetite is unusual," said Colin.

"On the contrary, you're looking much better! Your father would be pleased to hear the news."

"Don't tell my father! If you do, I'll stop eating completely!"

Stunned, the doctor decided not to tell Colin's father. He had a talk about it with Mrs. Medlock and decided to let Colin and Mary laugh.

CHAPTER 22

"It's Mother!"

Magic was a very serious matter to Colin, Mary, Ben, and Dickon. After the chantings one midsummer morning, while the three youngsters were in the garden, Colin stood up, raised his hands above his head, and shouted, "I'm well!" He jumped once, twice, and yelled, "I'm going to live forever! I'm all better!"

He turned to Mary and Dickon. "Do you remember how I was when you first got me here? I could hardly jab the spade into the earth! Now I can do that and a whole lot of digging without strain! It's a marvelous feeling! I've grown stronger."

After a moment, Dickon said, "There's a song we sing in church. Mother says skylarks wake up every morning singing it. May I sing it for you?"

At Colin's excited nod, Dickon took off his cap and sang in a strong, true voice:
"Praise God from whom
All blessings flow,
Praise Him all creatures here below,
Praise Him above all ye Heavenly Host,
Praise Father, Son, and Holy Ghost.
Amen."

When he finished, Colin spoke to him: "I like it! Nice song. It suits me well. I want to shout out that I'm thankful to magic. This is my song. Can you help us sing it?"

Dickon took them through it several times. And they sang it again. Mary and Colin lifted their voices as musically as they could, and Dickon's swelled quite loud and beautiful. At the second line Ben Weatherstaff raspingly cleared his throat, and at the third line he joined in with great vigor. Mary observed that Ben, like Colin, had tears in his eyes when he found that he was not a cripple.

Suddenly Colin looked across the garden. "Who is that woman by the door?"

"It's Mother!" exclaimed Dickon as he ran full speed toward her. Colin and Mary followed. So this was Mrs. Sowerby! They smiled at her kind and fresh face. The children took her to see the garden. Colin looked into her eyes and said softly, "Even when I was sick, I wanted to see you."

The sight of his uplifted face brought about a sudden change in her own. She flushed and the corners of her mouth shook and a mist seemed to sweep over her eyes.

"Me too!" squealed Mary. "Martha's told me so much about you."

The Secret Garden

"I've heard about this place for so long, I feel like I've been here forever," said Mrs. Sowerby.

"Are you surprised to see me so well?" asked Colin.

"Truly, I am! You look so much like your mother, it startled me. I remember your mother quite well, lad."

"Will my father like me now?"

"Why wouldn't he?" replied Ben. "Look at him, Susan Sowerby. Colin's legs have become strong trunks in just two months!"

Mrs. Sowerby turned to Mary and said, "You look well, too, Miss Mary. I'll bet you look like your mother. Martha told me that she was said to be quite the beauty!"

Hearing her say that she was as beautiful as her mother, Mary flushed with pure pleasure. Dickon's mother walked around the garden and looked at each plant and leaf. She praised their decorations and arrangements. She was quite an easy woman to talk to, with a quick and warm laugh.

She spent a good hour with Ben and the children. Colin and Mary bombarded her with questions regarding her large brood of children. She was more than happy to answer them all. The garden enclosure was filled with their laughter.

When it was time for them all to leave, Colin caught her hand and looked at her with absolute adoration.

"I wish you were my mother as well," he said. He then gave her a warm hug. Her eyes filled with tears as she hugged him back.

"Oh, my boy. Your mother is right here in this garden, watching over you. Your father must come back and see you now. He'll surely be glad of the changes!"

CHAPTER 23

Archibald Craven

To let a sad thought or a bad one get into your mind is as dangerous as letting a scarlet fever germ get into your body. If you let it stay there after it has got in you, it may never get out as long as you live.

As long as Mary had disagreeable thoughts about herself, she'd remain a sickly, unattractive girl. As long as Colin thought he was going to die, he'd remain a little half-crazed boy. But the changes that came along in both Mary and Colin were unbelievable! While the secret garden was coming alive and the children along with it, Archibald Craven, Colin's father, was wandering in far-off places. He visited beautiful places in Europe. Yet he was gloomy and miserable.

One day, he was in the Tyrolean countryside in Austria, a place whose beauty could lift even the darkest of souls! He found a clump of beautiful blue forget-me-nots blooming in great profusion. That was enough to put some light into his darkness-filled heart.

On his way home, he noticed his legs were less heavy and his shoulders less burdened. He sat and stared at the bright delicate blueness. Time stood still! He did not know what was happening to him. At last he moved as if he were awakening. He got up slowly and stood on the moss carpet, drawing a deep breath. Something seemed to have been unbound and released in him, very quietly.

"What is it?" he said, almost in a whisper, and he passed his hand over his forehead. "I almost feel as if I were alive!" He slept much better, not being troubled by nightmares. He felt stronger. He even thought of Misselthwaite Manor and Colin and wondered if he should go back.

One day in his dream he heard a sweet, familiar voice: "Archie! Archie!"

"Lilias! Where are you? Answer me!"

"In the garden, Archie, in the garden."
The voice faded away and he woke up with a start. He noticed a couple of letters on his desk. Among them was Mrs. Sowerby's. She had written he must come home quickly. "I've no doubt of the joy you'll feel when you return and see the children," she wrote.

He read the letter a few more times and remembered the dream.

"I'm going back," he said almost immediately. "I'm going home, at once!"

CHAPTER 24

In the Garden

In a few days, he was back in England, arriving by train to Yorkshire. On his long railroad journey he found himself thinking of his boy as he had never thought of him in all of the ten years past.

"Perhaps I have been all wrong for ten years," he said to himself. "Ten years is a long time. It may be too late to do anything now. What have I been thinking!"

He was calm and happy as the carriage drove across the moor. He felt a sense of homecoming when the great manor house came into view. He remembered his dream and the sound of his beloved's voice. It had felt so good!

"In the garden," the voice had said. But the key was buried long ago, and he didn't remember where exactly. He made up his mind to go hunt for it the moment he got home.

When he arrived, he headed straight for the library and rang for Mrs. Medlock. She came running in, flustered and flushed. Before she could speak, he asked, "How is Colin?"

"Well, uh, sir, he's different," she said.

"Has he become weaker?"

"On the contrary, sir! None of us knows how it's happened. He wouldn't eat. He'd have those horrible tantrums. Then he met Mary, the girl from India, and things changed! She shouted at him once for screaming, and he's kept quiet since! He goes out each day, and his appetite's increasing. He's put on a few pounds."

"Where does he go, Mrs. Medlock?"

"Always in the garden, sir."

"In the garden . . ." He thought of his dream and left the library immediately. His long strides took him down the paths Mary had first walked, through the kitchen gardens, and then along the ivy-covered wall. He remembered how he had buried the key in rage and grief after his wife died. The ivy was so thick and full, it could take a while before he found the door.

No human being had passed that portal for ten lonely years, and yet inside the garden there were sounds of running, scuffling feet. There were strange sounds of lowered, suppressed voices, of smothered, joyous cries like the laughter of young things and the uncontrollable laughter of children who were trying not to be heard.

He looked around but saw no one. The voices grew louder and the footsteps clearer. The door in the wall was flung wide open, the sheet of ivy swinging back. A boy burst through it at full speed and dashed almost into his arms.

Mr. Craven steadied both of them, and gasped for breath. He looked at the boy as the boy looked at him. The boy was tall and handsome. He was glowing with life. His running had sent splendid color leaping to his face. He threw the thick hair back from his forehead and lifted a pair of strange gray eyes full of boyish laughter, rimmed with black lashes. It was the eyes that made Mr. Craven gasp for breath. "Who? Who?" he stammered.

The boy looked at the man, drew himself to his full height, and said in a soft, yet strong voice, "Father, it's me, Colin."

His father said hurriedly, "In the garden! In the garden!"

"Yes," said Colin. "It was the garden that did it, along with Mary, Dickon, the creatures, and the magic. We kept the secret to tell you when you returned from your trip. I'm well. I can beat Mary in a race. I'm going to be an athlete."

He said it all so like a healthy boy— his face flushed, his words tumbling over one another in his eagerness—that Mr. Craven's soul shook with unbelieving joy.

Colin put out his hand and laid it on his father's arm. "Aren't you glad, Father?" he asked. "Aren't you glad? I'm going to live forever!"

Mr. Craven put his hands on both the boy's shoulders and held him still. "Take me into the garden, my boy," he said at last. "And tell me all about it."

And so they led him in. The place was a wilderness of autumn gold, purple, violet blue, flaming scarlet! On every side there were bunches of white and ruby lilies blooming in late glory! Roses climbed and hung clustered, and the sunshine

deepening the hue of the yellowing trees made one feel as though he were standing in a temple of gold. Mr. Craven stood silent and looked around.

Then they sat down under their tree—all but Colin, who wanted to stand while he told the story.

It was the strangest thing he had ever heard, Archibald Craven thought. It poured forth in headlong boy fashion. Mystery, magic, and wild creatures! And the coming of spring, the passion of insulted pride that had dragged Colin to his feet to defy old Ben Weatherstaff! The odd companionship, the great secret so carefully kept!

Mr. Craven laughed until tears came into his eyes, sometimes tears also came when he was not laughing. The athlete, the lecturer, the scientific discoverer was a laughable, lovable, healthy, young human being.

"And that," said Colin, "is the end of my story. Come, Father. I shall walk back to the house with you."

Mrs. Medlock gave a little shriek. Every person bolted across the servants' hall and stood looking with astonishment!

Across the lawn came the master of Misselthwaite and he looked as many of them had never seen him. And by his side with his head up in the air and his eyes full of laughter walked as strongly and steadily as any boy in Yorkshire—Master Colin.

About the Author

Frances Hodgson Burnett was an English-American playwright and author. She was born in Cheetham Hill, Manchester, England on November 24, 1849. Her father died in 1854, and her family had to live in absolute poverty in the Victorian slums. After her mother's death in 1867, eighteen-year-old Frances was the head of the family with four younger siblings to support.

She began writing and published her first story in *Godey's Lady's Book* in 1868. Her main writing talent was combining realistic detail of working-class life with a romantic plot.

The Secret Garden was written in 1909 and is the children's novel for which she is still best known today.

The Adventures of Tom Sawyer
The Adventures of Pinocchio
Alice in Wonderland
Anne of Green Gables
Beauty and the Beast
Black Beauty
The Call of the Wild
A Christmas Carol
Frankenstein
Great Expectations
Journey to the Center of the Earth
The Jungle Book
King Arthur and the Knights of the Round Table
Little Women
Moby Dick
The Night Before Christmas and Other Holiday Tales
Oliver Twist
Peter Pan
The Prince and the Pauper
Pygmalion
The Secret Garden
The Time Machine
Treasure Island
White Fang
The Wind in the Willows
The Wizard of Oz